OUT OF THE RUBBLE

SALLY NICHOLLS

XFORD
VERSITY PRESS

gton Stoke

OXFORD
UNIVERSITY PRESS

Great Clarendon Street, Oxford, OX2 6DP, United Kingdom

Oxford University Press is a department of the University of Oxford.

It furthers the University's objective of excellence in research, scholarship, and education by publishing worldwide. Oxford is a registered trade mark of Oxford University Press in the UK and in certain other countries

© Sally Nicholls 2022

Additional resources © Oxford University Press 2022

The moral rights of the author have been asserted

First published in 2022

British Library Cataloguing in Publication Data
Data available

978-0-19-849495-9

978-1-38-202904-9 (ebook)

10 9 8 7 6 5 4 3 2 1

Paper used in the production of this book is a natural, recyclable product made from wood grown in sustainable forests.

The manufacturing process conforms to the environmental regulations of the country of origin.

Printed in Great Britain by CPI Group (UK) Ltd., Croydon CR0 4YY

Acknowledgements

Cover illustration by Daniela Jaglenka Terrazzini

The publisher would like to thank the following for permission to reproduce photographs and other copyright material: ... We have tried to trace and contact all copyright holders before publication. If notified, the publisher will be pleased to rectify any errors or omissions at the earliest opportunity.

To my mum

Chapter 1

The Station

The train pulled in to Paddington Station on a grey evening in early February.

The journey had taken nearly all day. The train kept starting and stopping. A whole troop of soldiers got on at Bath and filled the compartment, laughing and shouting. Judy didn't mind. She was used to soldiers.

It was five and a half years since Judy had left London. She looked out of the train window now, trying to get a sense of what it was like. Everything looked grey and cold and dark. There were big stone houses, lots with boarded-up windows. She saw a half-destroyed block of flats with all of its beams showing on one side, like wooden bones.

London looked a bleak, rundown sort of place, Judy thought. This was supposed to be a home-coming. But it didn't feel like home at all.

The lady in the seat opposite smiled at Judy. "Are you an evacuee?" she said.

Judy nodded. "Mum got sick of waiting for the end of the war and said I could come home," she explained. "She sent me a telegram when we won the Battle of the Bulge. The Germans are retreating. There's hardly any bombing any more, she said."

"My boys are coming home next week," the lady told her. "I can hardly wait! Five years they've been away." She smiled at Judy again. "Excited?" she asked.

Was Judy excited? She wasn't sure. She'd been sent away in 1939 when she was nine. She'd lived in Somerset with two old ladies, Auntie Betty and Auntie Poll. They weren't her real aunties – that was just what she'd called them. They were best friends who lived together in a small cottage with a straw roof and chickens in the garden. The house looked like something in a storybook.

Judy couldn't remember being sad to leave Mum and Dad. She remembered being nervous, but mostly she remembered how *exciting* it had been. Like going on a really, really long holiday. Her parents had always loved and looked after her, and Judy had taken it for granted that the aunties would love her and look after her too. And they had.

Auntie Betty and Auntie Poll didn't know much about children. But they were kind. They showed Judy how to make bread and how to pluck a chicken. They helped her write letters to her mother and father. They had saved their butter rations to make cakes for her birthdays and invited her friends round for buns and party games when she'd been younger.

The rooms in the aunties' cottage were small and dark. There was no electricity, and there were mice in the roof. There were oil lamps in the living room, and Judy had to take a candle up to bed. If she needed a wee in the night, she had to use the pot under the bed.

But there was a garden with foxgloves and hollyhocks and ox-eye daisies, and potatoes and carrots and cabbages. There were fresh eggs for tea, and a tiny village school with two rooms. Their milk was delivered on the back of a cart pulled by a real horse. Judy had missed Mum and

Dad, of course. But she had loved the little town right from the start.

Auntie Betty and Auntie Poll had nearly been crying when they'd put Judy on the train that morning.

"Send us a postcard when you get to London," Auntie Betty said.

"Don't forget the eggs and the butter in your basket," said Auntie Poll. "Give them to your mum straight away. There's never as much food in cities."

"All right," said Judy. The whole thing felt very strange. Would she ever see the aunties again? She didn't know how she was supposed to feel. Sad to be leaving? Happy to be going back to live with Mum? Could you be happy and sad and nervous and excited all at the same time? Judy didn't know. Not knowing made her feel awkward and cross. Fortunately, Auntie Betty seemed to understand.

"Well," she said. "Goodbye, darling. Give our love to your mum."

And that was that.

"I bet your mum can't wait to see you," the lady on the train said to Judy.

4

Judy nodded. Her mum had come to visit whenever she could, but it was hard with her work. Often three or four months would pass without Judy seeing her. Mum wrote Judy a letter every week. Her dad wrote too, but not so often. He was a chaplain – a vicar at an air-force base in Brighton.

"The war will be over soon," said the lady. "Everyone says so."

"I know," said Judy. But she didn't really believe it. The war had been going on for so long, she couldn't remember what life had been like before it started.

The train was slowing down. Judy could see other tracks out of both windows, all heading towards different platforms. And suddenly, there they were! In the station. One of the soldiers got Judy's suitcase down from the rack for her.

"Can you see your mum?" asked the lady.

Judy looked out of the window. "Oh! Yes!" she said. Mum waved at Judy, and Judy stumbled out of the train. The soldier handed Judy her suitcase. And then Mum was hugging her and she was home.

Chapter 2

The Caravan

Home.

What did that mean – home? Judy had a picture in her head of what home was. It was being very small, sitting by the fireside on a Sunday evening, eating buttered toast with your mum and dad.

It was living in the same house as your family and knowing that the house was yours and nobody could take it away.

But Judy didn't have a home like that. Their house had been bombed in 1940, a few months after Judy had been sent away. Now Mum lived in a caravan in Uncle Jack's back yard. Because of the bombing, there weren't enough houses left for everyone to live in. Lots of people were homeless. Judy wondered where her family was going to end up. Her dad was a vicar. His church had been destroyed in the Blitz, so when he came out of the air force he'd have to find a new job. It could be anywhere.

It was cold when Judy and her mum came out of the station and beginning to rain. Judy shivered.

"It's not far to Uncle Jack's," said Mum. "Then we'll have a bit of tea. I bet you're hungry, aren't you? Look, there's a bus! Come on!"

The bus was full of people. It smelt of damp macintoshes, wet paper parcels, hair oil, petrol and sweat. There was a man in a sailor's uniform and an air-raid warden wearing a tin hat. There were no other children.

"The girls' school is still closed," said Mum. "But they're saying it might open soon. The boys' school is open, but I think it's only half full. The little school on the high street is open too, but you're too old for that."

Judy had gone to the grammar school in Somerset.

"It won't do you any harm to have a bit of time off," said Mum. She looked sideways at Judy and gave her a small smile. "It's just nice to have you back."

Judy smiled too. It *was* nice to be back, she supposed, but she didn't feel very glad about it.

Instead, Judy mostly felt empty. It was nice to see Mum, but she didn't feel like she'd come home. Did she even have a home any more? It was a strange and rather lonely thought.

"I've got you a present," Judy said suddenly, remembering the basket. "It's from Auntie Poll and Auntie Betty really."

Mum's smile disappeared. But she took the basket from Judy and looked inside. There were real eggs, strawberry jam, bacon and a little pat of butter. Judy and the aunties had thought so carefully about what Mum would like.

"The eggs come from our chickens," said Judy. "We've got four – all ladies. And the strawberries are from the garden. Auntie Betty and I made the jam together. We saved all our sugar ration for ages. The bacon is from Auntie Poll's brother – he's a farmer. And—"

"Yes, well," said Mum. She didn't look happy. "Things are different in the city. We can't all raise chickens."

Judy stopped, feeling hurt. Didn't Mum like the food?

"Auntie Poll—" Judy began. Mum interrupted.

"They aren't your aunties," she said. "It was very kind of them to look after you, but you're home now. You don't need to worry about them any more."

"But I'm not worried," said Judy, confused. "I like them. I liked living with them."

Mum's face dropped. Judy felt awful.

"I am glad I'm home," she said quickly.

Mum gave a small smile. "It'll be just like it always was," she said.

This was so untrue that Judy couldn't believe Mum had said it. How could it be just like it was? Judy was fourteen now, not nine. Dad was away at his air-force base. Everything was different. But Judy didn't say so. For the first time she felt like Mum was a child who needed protecting, and Judy was the grown-up.

"Just like it always was," Judy said, feeling a bit sick inside. Mum looked pleased.

Judy looked away, pretending to be very interested in what she could see out of the bus windows. London looked so different from the market town in Somerset where the aunties lived. It was so big! And so ... dirty. Everything looked tired and worn down. There were more houses with boarded-up windows. Rubbish in the gutters. Broken glass on the streets.

"Oh!" said Judy.

On the corner there was a bomb site. A pile of rubble where a house used to be. The back wall was still standing, but the rest of the house was a mess of broken planks, like a box of matchsticks.

"A real bomb site!" Judy said.

"There are lots of them in London," said Mum. "You get used to it. Look – there's the park. We used to go there when you were little."

Mum clearly didn't want to talk about the bomb site, so Judy didn't ask any more. But she couldn't stop thinking about the house. It looked so ... naked. So unprotected.

Did their old house look like that now?

They got off the bus soon after that and walked down the street where Uncle Jack lived.

"Couldn't you live in the house with Uncle Jack?" asked Judy. All of the houses on the street looked fairly big. Surely Uncle Jack must have a spare bedroom where Mum could live?

"No, thank *you*!" said Mum. "It's much nicer to have our own place." She stopped by a garden gate and put a key in the lock. "Come and see."

The back yard was small and dark. There were a couple of pots with dead plants in them. Some old paving slabs with dead weeds growing between the cracks. And there was the caravan.

It was an old-fashioned caravan, the kind that would have been pulled by a horse. It had a curved green canvas roof. The red walls were covered with yellow Romani patterns. The wheels and the steps up to the door were painted yellow. In the dark yard the caravan looked bright and cheerful, like a little piece of magic in a ruined city.

"It's beautiful!" said Judy, delighted.

Mum looked pleased. "It's rather lovely, isn't it?" she said. "Jack used to use it as an extra bedroom when he had guests."

"It's perfect!" said Judy. She had heard all about the caravan in her mum's letters, but she had never seen it. For the first time, being back in London seemed really exciting. "Oh, Mum!"

"It's a bit small," said Mum. "But it is fun."

Inside, the caravan *was* small, but everything was neat and clean. The curved roof made everything feel cosier. There was a little oil stove, a tiny kitchen, and a double bed at one end. There was a small wooden table with a bright yellow tablecloth and benches with padded cushions. There was even a bookshelf.

"The bench turns into a bunk too," said Mum. "It's a bit basic, but it's nice and warm next to the stove."

Mum bent down and lit the stove. "It takes a while to heat up," she said. "But once the stove gets going it's rather cosy."

There was a saucepan of stew on the gas ring. Mum warmed it up while Judy went to the house to wash her hands and face. The caravan had no running water, so they used the sink and toilet at Uncle Jack's house.

Mum and Judy ate the stew sitting at the small table. It was mostly vegetables, but Judy was used to that. She knew it was hard to make the meat ration stretch to many meals. There was no electricity in the caravan – just oil lamps, like in Auntie Poll and Auntie Betty's house. Judy liked that. The soft, orange light made her feel a bit more at home. She sat and looked around at the wooden walls. Home. This was home now.

It felt very strange.

"I'll have to go to work tomorrow," said Mum. "Will you be all right here on your own? You could go to the library if it's too cold. Or you could come into work with me, maybe? I'm sure you could help out if you wanted to."

Judy stared at her mum. She couldn't believe it. Judy had been away for years and years, and Mum was just going to go to work and leave her at home all on her own? Judy could feel tears starting behind her eyes – how awful! She couldn't cry. She looked away before Mum could see.

Mum worked in a National Restaurant. She cooked cheap food for people who didn't have much money. They made dinners for soldiers passing through London and people whose houses had been bombed.

Judy looked down at the table. She didn't know what to say. She hated the idea of being left on her own. But it would be worse to be in the Restaurant. It would be like being a child who couldn't look after herself. And everyone would be very kind and want to talk to her and give her jobs to do, and she wouldn't know what to say.

"No thanks," Judy said, trying to sound like she didn't care. "I'll be all right here on my own. I'm fourteen now, remember."

Fourteen was practically grown up. Lots of the girls from the village school had left school already and got jobs. Judy shouldn't mind being on her own all day. But she did. She didn't say so though. She wanted Mum to like her.

Mum looked relieved. "I've got some books you can read if you want," she said. "Or you could have an explore. I used to love riding the buses when I was your age."

"All right," said Judy. It wasn't Mum's fault, she thought. She couldn't help having to work.

"I'm sorry," said Mum. She did look sorry. "I wish I didn't have to work, but you won't be on your own for long. More children are coming back every day. I'm sure they'll open the girls' grammar school soon."

"It's OK," said Judy. She didn't want to make a fuss.

Mum said Judy could have the double bed.

"There's a curtain you can pull across – look," Mum said. "That way you'll get a bit of privacy. And there's a shelf here for your things."

"Thank you," said Judy. Mum was giving up her bed. Judy knew she should be grateful.

They went over to the house to clean their teeth and wash. Uncle Jack wasn't there. He volunteered as an air-raid warden, Mum said, so he was out all night.

"Are there still bombs?" asked Judy, alarmed.

"Sometimes," said Mum. "But hardly ever. Don't look so worried."

*

Back in the caravan, it was time for bed. With
the stove burning, the caravan was warm, much
warmer than Judy's bedroom at the aunties' house.
Judy climbed into bed and drew the curtain. Light
still came in through the gaps. The caravan smelt
of wood and wet mackintosh and brass polish
and stew.

This morning, Judy had been in her room in
Auntie Poll and Auntie Betty's house. Now she was
here. It felt like a thousand years had passed since
she'd woken up.

Judy lay listening for a long time. Mum was
pottering about, tidying up. Cars rumbled by on
the main road at the end of the street. People
walked past, talking and laughing. They didn't
seem bothered by the chance of bombs. But London
had been a dangerous place for so long that Judy
found it hard to relax. Would there be any bombs
tonight? She couldn't hear any aeroplanes or
sirens. But maybe they would come later?

Judy was still wondering this when she fell
asleep.

Chapter 3

The City

Judy woke up slowly the next morning. Her bed was warm and soft. The caravan smelt of frying bacon. "Love in Bloom" was playing on the wireless radio and her mum was singing along.

"Hello!" said Judy, poking her head out of the curtain.

Her mum turned and smiled. "Good morning! Oh, it is lovely to have you home."

Judy smiled back. It *was* nice. For a moment, she felt surprised.

The bacon was delicious, but the rest of breakfast wasn't. Mum was saving the aunties' eggs for a cake, so they had powdered eggs for breakfast. They tasted slimy and disgusting. To go with the eggs, they had National Loaf – wartime bread that tasted like sawdust.

"I'm sorry," said Mum. "It's so hard to make something nice with everything rationed …"

Judy nodded and tried not to mind, but she did. In the country, they always had fresh eggs.

After breakfast, they washed up and put everything away. Then Mum put on her coat and hat. "There's a London A to Z on the table," she said. "I thought you could come and have dinner in the National Restaurant. You could have lunch there too if you wanted? I've written down the address – it's not far. Do you think you'll be able to find it?"

"Of course," said Judy. "I can read a map."

"You could come and walk in with me now if you wanted," said Mum. She looked like she didn't want to leave.

"I'm *fine*," Judy said. "Really." All of a sudden, she was desperate for Mum to go. It felt like a million years since Judy had been properly on her own.

"You could have a bit of an explore maybe," Mum suggested.

"Good idea," said Judy. "Thanks."

Mum hesitated. "You will be all right, won't you?" she said.

"Definitely," said Judy. She wished Mum would just go. She was sick of smiling and looking pleased and telling her not to worry.

Mum nodded. She waved goodbye and shut the door.

Judy sat down at the table. She looked around the small caravan.

Now what?

She wrote a postcard to Auntie Poll and Auntie Betty:

Dear Auntie Poll and Auntie Betty,

How are you? I am fine. I have arrived safely in London. Mum says thank you for the food.

Judy stopped writing. What else could she say?

We are living in a caravan. I miss you.

Love from
Judy

Judy wrote the address on the postcard and stuck on a stamp. Auntie Poll and Auntie Betty had given her a whole sheet of stamps to send letters with. Then she looked in the kitchen cupboards.

There wasn't much. Some bread, some fruit. A bit of cheese. Judy made herself some sandwiches for lunch and put them in her rucksack. Then she went out.

The area where Uncle Jack lived was mostly rows of houses. Judy knew their old house had been near here, but she didn't remember any of these streets. They were full of biggish houses, with no gardens and hardly any trees. There was very little green at all. Everything was grey. Grey roads. Grey pavements. Grey houses. Grey rooftops. Grey sky.

It was very different from Somerset. There, everyone had gardens. If you walked five minutes from the aunties' cottage, you were surrounded by fields and trees. After school, Judy and her friends used to go and sit by the stream. They'd eat their sweet rations and flirt with the boys from the boys' grammar school.

Judy was surprised now by how much she missed the greenness of Somerset. It felt so odd to be surrounded by big tall houses in London. All of the chimneys were puffing out coal smoke, and the air was thick and sooty.

She walked slowly down the street, looking for something she remembered, but everything looked strange. Her old school had been around here somewhere, but Judy couldn't remember the name of the street it was on. Perhaps she could find it in the A to Z?

Judy passed a little park – she did remember that. She remembered playing on the swings and Mum pushing her on the roundabout. But the swings and the roundabout were gone now. They must have been taken away to be turned into bombs and aeroplanes, like the iron railings around the church in Somerset.

And then there were the bomb sites.

They were everywhere you went. The bombed streets reminded Judy of a mouth with teeth missing. She would be walking down an ordinary road of terraced houses and suddenly there would be a pile of rubble. Sometimes the whole house would be gone. Sometimes the front had been blown away but the rest was still there, shocking and naked, like a ruined doll's house.

You could still see the wallpaper on the walls.
Pictures with smashed glass. Broken furniture
still in the rooms. A bookcase full of water-logged
books. The bath and the sink and the toilet. It
made Judy shiver. It was like looking at the dead
body of a home.

She could see other signs of the war too. On
one street, there was a place where something
must have bounced along the pavement. Every
time it'd landed, it had made a crater and sent
long cracks out into the street. Judy followed the
trail, fascinated. What could the bouncing thing
have been?

At the end of the road, the thing must have
bounced into a terraced house and exploded. And
now there was no house there. Just a ruin. It had
been a bomb. A bouncing bomb. Judy shivered.

This was what she'd read about in
newspapers – the Blitz. She had seen pictures
of the bombing, of course, but there had been no
bombs in Somerset. No air raids. She'd had a very
safe, rather boring war. Being in London made the
whole thing seem very real.

Judy wondered what her old home looked like,
the one she and Mum and Dad had lived in. Did she
want to see it? She wasn't sure. Was it just a pile

of rubble? Or was any of it still standing? Could people look inside and see her old bedroom? She'd had a green bedspread, and a picture of rabbits on the wall, and a row of stuffed animals who lived at the bottom of her bed. She didn't like the idea of them all being buried in rubble. But what if people could look in and see them? Would that be worse?

She didn't know.

After wandering for a while, at last she came to a wider road, with buses and much grander houses. Judy was beginning to get cold, and she didn't want to go home, so she got on a bus. She still had two shillings left of her birthday money, which would buy a lot of bus tickets. She didn't mind where the bus was going. She just wanted to see a bit more of the city.

For the rest of the day, Judy sat on the top deck of the bus. She rode all the way to the end of the route, then back again. She was astonished by what she saw. All the big, grand buildings! They looked like palaces. The statues! So many people! When she was younger, she must have thought this was ordinary. But now it seemed amazing.

London, she thought. *This is home now.*

It was a strange thought.

Judy got off and ate her sandwiches in a little public garden at the end of the bus line, watching people going past. She would have liked to explore a bit, but she was worried about getting lost. Maybe tomorrow.

At five o'clock, the bus dropped her back on the small high street near Uncle Jack's house. The National Restaurant where Mum worked was in a community centre nearby. It wasn't hard to find.

But at the door of the Restaurant, Judy was suddenly shy again. Would Mum be too busy to talk to her? Would Judy have to talk to all the other ladies in the kitchen? Or would she have to eat her dinner on her own, with everyone looking after her? *Why* did Mum have to work? She never had before the war. She'd stayed at home and looked after Judy, and helped Judy's dad run the church.

But in the end, it was fine. The hall was full of long tables, but most of the customers weren't there yet. At one end of the room was a hatch that opened onto the kitchen. Mum was standing at the hatch wearing a big apron. She smiled and waved when she saw Judy.

"Judy!" Mum said. "Over here!"

There were three other ladies working there, and they were all delighted to see Judy.

"This can't be your daughter!" one lady said to Mum. "She's so grown up!"

"Oh, she looks just like you!" said another lady.

"Your mum's been so excited about you getting back, love," the first lady said.

Judy felt a bit awkward with them all clustered around her. But it was nice to feel so welcome.

All of the ladies wanted to tell Judy about their children.

"My grandsons are still in Wales," said one. "My daughter moved up there when the bombing started. She says she's not coming back until the war's over, but – oh! – I do miss them."

"My little girl's living with her auntie," another lady said. "They live by the seaside – she's having a lovely time. My daughter won't want to come home! I'd bring her back now if I could, but I'm so worried about the buzz-bombs. They still come over, you know."

Buzz-bombs were unmanned missiles – bombs that flew without a pilot. Hitler had started sending them over last year. They chugged over the countryside until they reached London and then they fell to the ground. Judy looked quickly at her mum, who said, "Goodness, there are hardly any buzz-bombs any more! I haven't heard one in weeks!"

"Quite right!" said another lady, who had curly black hair and bright red lipstick. "It's perfectly safe! My three children have been back for months!"

Judy realised that everyone's lives had been shaken up by the war. Somehow it was nice to know that it wasn't just her. She felt like she was a jigsaw sometimes. All the different pieces of her had been flung up into the air and they'd all landed in different places.

And now here I am, Judy thought. She still couldn't work out how she felt about that.

Chapter 4

The Church

That night, Judy lay awake for a long time. She could hear the sound of the rain pattering against the caravan roof. She could hear Mum moving about in the living space. A large part of Judy wanted to call out, to tell Mum she was awake. Perhaps they could have a cup of cocoa together and talk about how strange this whole thing was. How strange it was to be together again. How strange to have to build their family again from scratch.

Judy didn't move.

She had liked living with Auntie Poll and Auntie Betty. They were kind people, and she knew they loved her. Still, she had never felt like their house was home. In the evenings, they would say, "Go out and play now, darling; we're tired." Judy didn't mind this – she had lots of friends in the village and could always find something to do. But she did mind feeling like she was a bother. Like she didn't quite belong.

Judy always had to be careful not to make too much noise, not to break things, not to ask for anything too expensive. Once she had broken a vase and Mum had had to send the money to repair it. Another time, Judy had needed a new coat, and she'd had to wait until Mum could come and choose one for her.

The aunties' cottage wasn't quite a home, and it wasn't quite a hotel – it was sort of in between. Sometimes she was supposed to behave as if it was home, and sometimes she wasn't.

Judy had tried not to let it get to her. She had known that when the war was over, she would have a real home again.

But now here she was, and it wasn't at all like how Judy had imagined it. She and Mum were so shy of each other. Everything felt so unnatural. Judy felt like she didn't know any of the rules and was having to learn them all over again.

Despite the strangeness, Judy began to get used to living with her mum. The days were all very much the same. In the mornings, Mum would make them breakfast. Usually it was cereal, Cornflakes or Force or porridge. Sometimes they had powdered eggs or bacon as a special treat. Then Mum would rush out to work and Judy would be alone.

Sometimes she would try to read in the caravan, but it was always too cold. So Judy would put on her old coat and go out.

She would walk around the streets near Uncle Jack's house. She kept wondering about trying to find her old home, but something always stopped her. If it was raining, she would go to the library. And sometimes she would ride the buses around London, going further and further away each time.

The weekends were easier. On Saturdays, Judy and Mum would go on day trips. They went to Kew Gardens and Trafalgar Square and Buckingham Palace. You couldn't go inside Buckingham Palace, but you could look at the front. They watched the Changing of the Guards and afterwards Mum bought them some chocolate cake in a cafe. Judy was so tired of eating plain food every day that the cake was like magic. She ate hers slowly, savouring every spoonful.

On Sundays, they went to church and then had lunch with Uncle Jack in his big, cold, dark house. They had to give him their ration coupons before they ate, which always made Judy feel uncomfortable.

Uncle Jack was much older than Mum. They were very different people. Uncle Jack liked to complain, and he always seemed cross about something. Judy was glad they didn't live with him.

"How long are you two going to be squatting in my back yard?" Uncle Jack often grumbled.

Mum would always reply cheerfully. "Oh, not so long now," she'd say. "The war's nearly over! Dad will be home soon, won't he, Judy?"

But Judy hated hearing Uncle Jack talk like that.

"Why do we live here when he doesn't want us?" she said to Mum when they were back in the caravan.

"Uncle Jack doesn't mind really," Mum said. "He just likes to grumble."

But Judy minded. She hated feeling like she wasn't welcome.

Judy had been back for three weeks now. Nearly a month. She still didn't feel at home in London. But she was beginning to find more things that she liked. There were the nice ladies in the National Restaurant, who were always so pleased to see her. There was the way Mum always smiled when she came in the door, and their Saturday day trips. And there was London too. There were good things in London as well as bad things. Like the bomb sites.

There were bomb sites all across the city. Judy was fascinated by them. For one thing, they were the only place where there was any green. There weren't many flowers yet, of course, in March, but there was green. It felt like Nature had been waiting for the city to fall, and after the bombs, it was taking the land back. Most of the sites were covered in grass and small shrubby plants – wild gardens growing out of the broken earth.

Judy couldn't stop looking at the bomb sites. At first, she only looked. Gangs of boys played there after school, she knew. Judy often saw them climbing on the walls and chasing each other around the ruins. Sometimes she saw tramps and drunks and deserters from the military leaning against the walls, sharing a bottle of whisky between them. The tramps and the boys scared her a bit. Judy looked and looked, but she didn't explore.

And then she found it. *Her* bomb site. Home.

Judy found it quite by accident one day.
She had gone to the little high street nearby to
change her library books and spend her sweet
ration. Judy liked this high street. It was always
busy. The pavement was full of market stalls
selling old furniture and second-hand books.
There were people sitting on their front steps
smoking cigarettes and watching the world go
by. Newspaper boys called out the news. Soldiers
and sailors and air-force pilots walked around in
their uniforms, home on leave. Beggars sat on the
pavement, with dogs. So many people everywhere!

Judy bought herself a bag of toffees from the
grocer. Then she kept walking down the street.
There was a junction. Stop–go lights. A small bit
of green space with a couple of benches on it.

And the church. Dad's church.

Judy stood on the pavement and stared. The
church roof had been destroyed, but more than half
of the walls were still there, open to the sky. The
ground was a mess of rubble and broken pews and
splintered wood. A stone angel still stood watching
over the ruin, his face impossibly serious. A spider
had made a web between the angel's face and his

lifted arm. But even surrounded by the rubble, he looked calm and holy.

Judy opened the gate to the graveyard and went inside. The ground was thick with unmown grass. She walked carefully across it to the bell tower. There were fragments of glass and stone and wood still scattered among the grass. It wouldn't be wise to walk barefooted.

She stopped by the bell tower and looked up. One whole side of the tower had been blown away, but the other side was still standing. The bells had fallen and lay in the rubble, huge and solemn and half buried. Their round backs looked like sunken submarines, Judy thought. The bells were much bigger than she had expected. She would have liked to get closer, but there were large wooden boards saying DANGER and KEEP OUT.

Judy kept walking.

At the back of the churchyard was a small wooden gate. And behind the gate was the vicarage.

Home.

Judy felt oddly nervous. Her heart began to beat faster. Tingles ran up and down her arms. What would the house look like now? How much of it would still be there?

She took a deep breath and walked towards the gate. It looked just the same as she remembered.

When the bomb had fallen on the church, the blast had destroyed the front half of the vicarage too. All that was left was a messy pile of bricks and pipes and wires and broken planks.

Mum had been buried here, in the cellar she had used as a shelter. Judy stared at the pile of wreckage. It looked like an awful lot of weight to be trapped under. What had it felt like to be Mum in that moment? To feel a whole house coming down on top of you? It must have been terrifying.

Judy shivered. The Blitz felt very real suddenly, standing here now. Mum could easily have died. So many people had.

The back of the house was still standing. There was a kitchen, a living room, the spare bedroom and most of Judy's bedroom. Judy had not expected it to just be ... there. She came closer. The whole thing felt very unreal, like walking into a memory or a dream.

There was her bed. Her wallpaper, with little pink rosebuds on it. Her doll's house. She sat down, feeling overwhelmed. Here were the things she remembered, the happy house of her childhood. But also, here was plaster dust, mould, rain damage, damp. Here was broken glass and electric wires and water pipes and dirt. The real and the unreal, all muddled up together.

There were more DANGER notices all around the vicarage. Judy could see why. The whole house leaned sideways. The top floor bulged as if it was about to come crashing down. Most of the stairs were still there, but Judy could see how dangerous it would be to climb them. It looked as if it would have toppled just from the vibrations of a heavy lorry passing in the street. No wonder that part hadn't been raided by looters.

Judy came closer, until she was right on the edge of the pile of rubble. There were signs of life here too. Yellow wallpaper flapping from a fallen wall. A picture of a garden with a smashed frame. There was a lot of glass about. Someone had put tape across the windows to stop them breaking, but it hadn't really worked.

There was something poking out of the rubble. Judy bent to look. It was a stuffed toy – a rabbit, perhaps? She lifted the bricks aside and pulled, and the toy came out. A panda. It was soaking wet, filthy and rather squashed. Its stuffing was coming out of a hole in its tummy. It had a bit of blue ribbon around its neck and a rather daft expression.

This must have been Judy's panda once. It did look a bit familiar. She remembered the pile of soft toys on the end of her bed, but not this one. She brushed the dirt off the toy as best she could. She felt like an archaeologist – like Howard Carter discovering the tomb of King Tutankhamun.

Once upon a time, Judy had lived here. She could only half remember it. What had it really been like? What secrets were hiding here?

If she dug deeper, what would she find?

Chapter 5

The Ruin

That evening, Judy sat and watched Mum. Mum always seemed to look tired. They worked her hard at the Restaurant.

"Penny for your thoughts?" said Mum.

"Was it awful, being buried under the house?" Judy asked.

Mum looked surprised.

"Well, it wasn't much fun," she said. "But it was a long time ago. There's no point worrying about it now."

Judy supposed there wasn't. But after going to the house today, she had realised for the first time how strange it was not to talk about it.

"But what was it *like*?" she said.

Mum looked cross, which was odd. Sometimes Mum got quiet and tense. Sometimes she was happy. And sometimes, like Judy, she tried very hard to look happy even when she wasn't. But Mum wasn't often cross.

"Goodness, Judy, what do you think it was like?" Mum said. "Honestly! And take your shoes off the bench – look at that great big muddy mark on the cushion!"

Judy took her feet down. She was rather surprised. Mum didn't normally tell her off.

"Go and get some water and clean that mud off!" said Mum. "There's a bucket in that cupboard there – hurry up!"

Judy got the bucket and went over to Uncle Jack's kitchen to fill it up with water. She came back and washed the mud off the bench, then Mum said she was going to have a bath. And after that, Judy didn't feel like she could ask Mum about the bombing any more.

That night, something strange happened. Judy woke up and heard her mum crying.

It wasn't a gentle sort of crying, but a shuddering, gasping, desperate sort of sobbing. It scared Judy. This wasn't the sort of noise she expected Mum to make. Mums should be calm and happy. They should know what they were doing. They shouldn't sob and sob like the world was ending.

Judy lay there for a long time, listening. She wondered if she should go and give Mum a hug. Perhaps she should make a cup of tea and tell Mum everything was all right. That was the sort of thing mums and daughters did, wasn't it?

But Judy didn't move. Mum's crying felt too private, and Judy felt too shy. She didn't feel like she knew Mum well enough to help.

At last the noise stopped. But it was a very long time before Judy went back to sleep.

After that, Judy went back to the bombed vicarage every day.

She spent most of her time there, digging about in the ruins. At first, it hurt her hands, and once she cut her finger pretty badly on a piece of glass. That evening, Judy went rummaging in the coat cupboard at Uncle Jack's house. She found an old pair of gardening gloves and took them with her. That made things easier.

Mum was curious about what Judy did every day. She could tell. Judy would go to the public toilets on the high street and wash the dust off her hands and face, but she could never get all of it off. Fortunately, London *was* dusty and dirty, but Mum must have wondered. She never asked Judy about it though.

Mum and Judy were very careful around each other all the time. Judy was careful not to complain about being left on her own. She was careful never to say that she missed the countryside. When letters from Auntie Poll and Auntie Betty arrived, Judy was careful not to look too pleased. She put them in her pocket and saved them to read later. She was always very polite and she never complained about anything. Judy wanted Mum to like her. She wanted this new home to work.

"It's only Spam and potatoes for dinner," Mum said one Saturday. She never cooked much on weekends. "It's so hard to get food in a city."

"I don't mind," Judy said at once. "I like Spam." She didn't, much. But Judy knew Mum worried about living in a caravan and leaving Judy on her own. So she tried extra-hard to be nice about it.

Mum was trying too. Auntie Betty and Auntie Poll were nice, but they'd often get cross with Judy over little things like not shutting the back door or leaving dirty plates in her bedroom. Mum hardly ever got cross about anything Judy did. She didn't complain if Judy was late to dinner. She didn't complain if Judy forgot to do the washing-up or left her clothes on the floor, even though you had to be very tidy in the caravan. Mum was very polite, all the time.

It was hard work, always having to be on your best behaviour. Judy wished Mum would get angry sometimes. She didn't like having to guess what Mum was thinking. It was like being at a stranger's house.

It wasn't like a home.

The ruined vicarage wasn't home either – not any more. But Judy was always finding things in the rubble. A china shepherdess that was missing an arm but otherwise perfect. A wooden love spoon that Dad had made for Mum. Old books. Judy remembered the shepherdess – it used to sit on the mantelpiece in the living room. But most of the other things she had forgotten. How awful. To forget your own home.

A lot of the bomb site had been looted already. Judy knew that gangs of boys liked to collect bits of bombs, and often hunted on the sites for new pieces

to add to their collections. Once, Judy had seen boys
from the local grammar school charging towards
the ruins. They were waving flags and shouting,
and seemed to be playing some sort of wargame.

Judy hurried away before they saw her. But
when she came back the next day, she could see the
marks where they had been. There were the ashes
of a fire in the ruins. Chalk writing on the wall of
the church. Ginger-ale bottles and the wrapper
from a bar of Dairy Milk. The remains of a den.

"Little rotters!" Judy muttered. She picked up
the litter and rubbed at the writing on the wall
with her handkerchief. It took a bit of work, but it
came away in the end. Judy was surprised at how
angry she felt. This house was *hers*. It felt rather
horrible to think of other people playing here
and looking at all their things. But at the same
time, Judy could of course understand why boys
would want to come here. There was something
rather wonderful about the bomb sites. They were
neither one thing nor another.

As March slowly turned into April, Judy began to
notice other things. Life was beginning to come
back to the ruins. Every day there was something

different. Flowers grew between the cracks in the stonework. Tall pink stems of bombweed pushed up between the cracks in the stone. Little pink-white flowers called London Pride. A buddleia bush where the church altar would have been. Nettles, of course. And blackberry thorns, just like the bushes in the aunties' garden. The blackberry bushes were like a promise. Soon there would be flowers. Then fruit.

Soon the war would be over.

There were birds everywhere too. London birds: sparrows and pigeons and blackbirds. Once, Judy found a nest of baby mice, all pink and squeaking. There was a ginger cat who liked to sleep on the gravestones, and a little black and white stray cat who sometimes let Judy stroke him.

If it wasn't raining, Judy usually spent her morning digging through the ruins. At lunchtime, she ate her sandwiches and drank her Thermos flask of tea. Sometimes she would spend her sweet ration in a little shop on the high street, sucking each square of chocolate until it was gone. Sometimes Judy would explore the ruins, climbing on the walls or reading the names on the old gravestones. She hardly ever saw anyone else there.

Until the day Alan came.

Chapter 6
The Graveyard

It was early April when Judy saw Alan for the first time. The caravan was getting warmer, but it was still very cold in the mornings. Judy ate breakfast with her coat on, sitting right next to the stove.

Judy's mum was still worried about her, Judy could tell.

"What do you do all day on your own?" Mum asked Judy as she stirred the porridge. This was unusual. Normally Mum tried very hard not to pry.

"Nothing much," Judy said. "Just wander around and look at things."

"I could ask Uncle Jack if he'd let you come into the house," said Mum. "It's hard keeping the caravan warm with coal on the ration. But—"

"Eugh," said Judy. "No thank you! I like looking around. I missed all the Blitz, being evacuated."

She tried to explain what she meant so that Mum would understand. "Everyone in London had this huge thing happen to them. And I missed it. And I come back and there's this whole ruined city … It's so strange."

"Well …" said Mum. "If you're sure." But she didn't sound convinced.

Judy was in a good mood as she walked to the church. The sun was shining. The day felt brighter already. There was a springtime feel to the air. Soon the mornings would be warm again. Soon Judy would be going back to school.

The news about the war was good. There hadn't been any bombs in ages. The Allies were advancing further across Europe every day. Soon the war would be over.

Soon her dad would be home.

Judy was bouncing a little as she walked through the graveyard. She almost wanted to sing.

And then she saw him.

There was a boy lying on his stomach on a tombstone. He was holding a set of binoculars and pointing them towards the ruined vicarage. He looked about Judy's age, or a bit older. He was wearing an old brown coat, grey school socks and a grey grammar-school cap. School uniform.

So why wasn't he at school?

There was a satchel on the tombstone beside him. It was half open. A school exercise book poked out of the top. Was he bunking off? Judy moved closer, slowly.

"I do know you're there, you know," the boy said, pushing himself up.

Judy stepped back. "Oh! I'm sorry! I didn't mean—"

"It's OK," the boy added. He had thin, mousy hair and a narrow face. A clever face that was wary and rather amused. "You'd make a pretty rotten hunter though. Didn't anyone ever tell you not to step on twigs?"

"I wasn't hunting you!" Judy said. "I was just … I didn't know anyone else came here. In the day, I mean. Shouldn't you be in school?"

"Shouldn't you?"

"The girls' grammar isn't open yet," said Judy. "And I'm too old for the school on the high street."

"Oh. Lucky you."

"You're bunking off, aren't you?" said Judy.

The boy looked defensive. "Not exactly. I'm fourteen. I don't have to be in school. I've left."

"Why are you wearing a uniform then?" said Judy.

He pulled a face. "I haven't told my family yet."

"Oh."

"Yep," the boy said, and shook his head sorrowfully. "I had to pass all these exams to get into grammar school, so it's rather a big deal. They think I'm going to go to university. But I want to work with animals. I was evacuated to the New Forest to live with a chap who was a birdwatcher." He looked wistful.

"When did you get back to London?" said Judy. It was lovely to be talking to someone her own age again. She hadn't realised how much she'd missed it.

"Oh, ages ago. I only stayed a couple of months, then Mum called me back. She said she missed me too much. I was here for the whole Blitz."

"Crikey." Judy looked at him with respect. "What was it like?"

"It was ..." the boy began. He stopped. "Well, it was the Blitz, you know. Bombs and that."

"I suppose so." Judy felt a bit foolish to have asked. But nobody *talked* about the bombs. It felt so strange to be back here in this ruined city. Everyone else had lived through this huge and terrible thing while she'd been drinking milk and picking apples with Auntie Poll and Auntie Betty. Judy was grateful not to have lived through the bombing, but she couldn't help feeling like everyone else had shared this great ... *event*, and she was coming back to it as a stranger.

"I was in Somerset," Judy said. "I've only been back a month or so." She smiled at him. She suddenly wanted, very much, to have him as a friend. "I'm Judy."

"Alan."

"What were you looking at, Alan?"

"Black redstarts," he replied. "I *think* they've got a nest."

"*Really?*" Judy was thrilled. "A birds' nest! Where?"

"I'm not sure. They keep trying to distract me. See?"

"Oh, *yes!*" Judy said, and she could. There was a little black bird, about the size of a robin, fluttering about in the trees.

"They hardly ever nest in this country," said Alan. "Mostly they just fly over Britain on their way to China. I saw them yesterday and I looked them up in my bird book. I was *sure* they were redstarts. They like bomb sites. I *think* they have

47

a nest in the old vicarage somewhere. They keep trying to get me away from it."

"The vicarage? Is that safe? Boys come and play here sometimes. Won't they bother them?" Judy said.

"Only if they spot them," Alan replied. "The nest is pretty hidden, I think. Look!"

The little bird came out again, followed by another.

"They're a breeding pair!" said Alan.

"How gorgeous," said Judy. "I wish I could make myself a home out of sticks."

"Rather nice if you could," Alan agreed.

The birds disappeared into the hedges, looking for twigs. "What are you doing here?" Alan asked. "Are you birdwatching?"

"Oh! No. I'm just ..." How would Judy explain? "I used to live in the vicarage," she said. "When I was a kid. My dad was the vicar."

"Oh," Alan said. He didn't seem surprised.

"I was in Somerset when it got bombed," Judy said. "But my mum was here. They had to dig her out of the ruins. I just ..." She stopped. It felt odd to be talking about something so personal with a stranger. But also nice to say it out loud.

"This was my home," Judy went on. "It's where Mum and Dad and I used to live. And there's so much I've forgotten about it."

She looked at Alan to see if he was going to laugh.

"You want to remember," he said.

"Yes. That's it exactly. And I thought ... well, Mum never talks about it. Being bombed out, I mean. But she lost everything. All our photographs, all our books and furniture – everything. I mean, I did too, but it was different for me because I was in Somerset. I'd sort of lost it already. So I thought perhaps I could find some of the things that she lost and maybe ..."

Judy stopped, wondering what Alan would say. But he just nodded.

"I wouldn't go up to the top floor," he said. "Those beams look pretty rotten. I probably wouldn't go in the downstairs part either. But you should be all right looking through the rubble. I don't know how much is left though. Lots of people like to come and pick through ruins." Alan saw her face. "Sorry."

"No, I know they do," Judy said. Boys and tramps and deserters and all the other lost people of London, looking through her home.

"I still like it here," she said quickly. "I miss the countryside. London's so *grubby*. Where I lived in Somerset, we had a garden, and a little wood at the end of the lane ..."

"This isn't proper countryside, of course," said Alan. "It's scrub."

"Well, yes." Judy stopped, feeling foolish again. She felt rather defensive of her bomb site. "But there's lots of life here."

"Oh, yes," Alan agreed. "There always is in scrub. Much more than in forests, actually. All this new land to colonise – plants love it. And animals."

"How strange," said Judy. "You'd think it would be the opposite." But she could see that Alan was right. The old church was full of small birds flying in and out of the open roof space. There were flowers and small shrubs everywhere.

"When you smash something up, it just makes space for something new," Alan said. "Nature's like that."

"Lucky for us," said Judy, and smiled at him.

After a moment's hesitation, Alan smiled back.

The day was much better with Alan in it. Judy showed him all around the church, pointing out her favourite places. She was a more daring climber with Alan there. It wasn't sensible to climb too high when you were on your own – you needed a buddy. Judy had read enough books about girls getting lost up mountains to know that. It wasn't difficult climbing – the stairs up the bell tower were still more or less there. But it was dizzying to be up so high.

Alan was a pretty fair climber, and he didn't seem to get dizzy.

"If this was your staircase at home, you'd walk up it without thinking," he said.

"I wouldn't," said Judy. "I don't have a staircase. We live in a caravan."

"Really?" Alan sounded interested.

"Uh-huh." Judy nodded. "A proper old-fashioned caravan. I love it."

The staircase was made of stone. It curled in a spiral, like a seashell. Only one wall of the tower had blown away. Half of the staircase felt very normal and safe and enclosed, while the other half hung out in thin air. And even here, on bare stone, there were small plants. Moss and lichen covered the stones, and tiny yellow flowers poked out of the cracks in the stonework. It was amazing really,

Judy thought. How little life needed to survive. Even just a stone wall.

And then they were at the top of the tower. Judy could see the city spreading out below them. The high street. The school. It must be break-time – the children were out in the playground. There was a sea of slate rooftops. And the smoke from a thousand chimneys drifted up into the sky.

"It's beautiful," she said.

"It's not bad," said Alan. "I'm going to bring my camera next time. You could get some pretty decent photos from up here."

"You've got a camera?" Judy was impressed.

"It was my dad's," said Alan. There was something about his voice. Judy could tell he didn't want to talk about it. But Judy felt a smile curling up her mouth. He had said "next time"! He was coming back!

They sat together for a while, looking out. The city looked so different from above. Judy spotted a rubbish tip. A house with a huge garden. A red bus full of shoppers. And of course there – and there – and there – and there – were the bomb sites. They looked incredible from above. Huge flattened ruins in the middle of a great city. Poor battered London. Judy shivered. It was cold up here.

"It must have been awful, the Blitz," she said, looking sideways at Alan. She wasn't prepared to let the subject go so easily.

Alan shrugged. "Some bits were nice," he said. "People used to sing in the bomb shelters. I liked that."

"Wasn't it dangerous?" Judy asked.

Alan gave another shrug. "We slept in the Underground. That wasn't so bad."

He was just like Mum. Didn't people want to talk about the bombings? Judy was sure that she would, if she'd been there. She was always wanting to talk about Auntie Poll and Auntie Betty. She hated how stiff Mum got when she mentioned them. She *missed* them. It felt wrong, pretending the aunties didn't exist.

Judy and Alan spent the rest of the day exploring the ruins. They climbed to the top of the big rubble heap. They explored the little chapel at the side of the church. The altar was still there, buried under the rubble. It made Judy feel rather strange to see it just lying there forgotten.

"There used to be silver plate and things," said Judy. "Mum said they got most of it out, but people came in and stole some of it. Isn't that awful?"

Alan shrugged. "Better it gets used than just sits here and rots."

"But it belonged to the church!" said Judy, rather shocked. "They would have used it."

Alan shrugged again. "I don't know what silver plates have to do with God," he said. "If God is anywhere, He's in ... flowers and trees and birds and things. Not treasure."

Judy was silent. She didn't know how to answer this. She loved all the ritual of the church – the candles and the robes and the singing. But Alan was right that if God was anywhere, He was here in the lovely wilderness.

They ate their lunch together sitting on one of the broken walls. Alan had meat-paste sandwiches and an apple, and a hard-boiled egg with salt in a little twist of paper. He had a Thermos with tea in it. Judy had Spam sandwiches, and two yellow pears, and digestive biscuits with margarine and hundreds and thousands on the top – a treat from Mum.

"You can have one if you want," she said.

Alan gave the biscuits a funny look. Did he think they were childish? Judy supposed they were, a bit. But he ate one all the same.

After lunch, Alan poked around the ruined church, peering into holes and climbing on top of walls. Judy left him to it. Alan seemed like someone who was happiest on his own. She carried on digging in the rubble of the old vicarage. After a while, he came and watched her.

"There are rats in the church," Alan said. "I think I found a nest. And their droppings are everywhere. No wonder there are so many cats."

"I don't mind rats," Judy said.

Alan seemed a bit surprised. "Why should you?" he said. "Rats are clever. Clean, too."

They looked at each other. Then Alan said, "School's getting out about now. I have to go. Otherwise they'll wonder where I am."

"OK."

A pause. Judy waited. Then she said lightly, "I'll probably be here tomorrow."

Alan nodded. "I want to come back with my camera," he said. "Get some shots of the church."

"Tomorrow then," said Judy.

Alan gave a sharp nod and was gone.

Chapter 7

The National Restaurant

The bomb site felt rather lonely after Alan had left. Judy stayed for a bit, but she didn't really feel much like digging any more. She decided to go to the National Restaurant and see Mum. Judy could always have a cup of tea while she was waiting for her to finish.

Mum was behind the counter when Judy came in. She wore a pink apron and a headscarf. She looked busy and happy.

"Look!" she said. "There's a letter from Dad! He's got some leave – he's coming to see us!"

Judy's dad didn't get much leave. Still, at least he was in England. Lots of Judy's friends had dads who were in Africa or Europe or Japan. Dad had come to Somerset a couple of times and Mum went down to visit him in Brighton sometimes. They were lucky, Judy knew.

"Oh!" she said. "Oh, Mum!" She felt the smile spread across her face. She could see the same thing happening to Mum – the same smile reflected back at her.

"How much leave does Dad have?" Judy asked.

"A couple of days," said Mum. "It'll be a bit of a squash in the caravan – I hope we'll be all right."

"We'll manage," said Judy. She smiled at her mum. Dad, home! They'd be a family again.

Perhaps when Dad was here, London would finally start to feel like home.

Judy waited in the National Restaurant while her mum finished serving the meals. She helped the ladies wipe down the tables and do the last of the washing-up.

"You're a war worker now," said Mum, and Judy smiled. She liked that idea.

It was dark when they headed back home together. Judy hummed to herself as she walked. She thought of Dad … Alan … springtime. Springtime … Alan … Dad.

"Happy?" said Mum, and Judy nodded.

She was.

The next morning, Judy got to the bomb site as early as she could. But Alan was already there.

He was standing on a tombstone, pointing his camera at the old church. His binoculars were hanging around his neck. Judy waved and Alan climbed down off the tombstone and came over to her.

"I got here just before breakfast," he said. "The light is best for photographs in the morning. I got some good shots of the church – at least, I think I did. I'll have to see what they look like when I've developed them."

"Have you got your own darkroom?" Judy asked.

"Uh huh. My dad built one in the box room. Maybe I'll go into the vicarage and take some photographs from the inside. What do you think?"

She stared at him. He lifted the camera and took a snapshot.

"Hey!" Judy said.

"Sorry, I couldn't resist! You looked so beautifully horrified. Don't worry, I didn't mean it. There were rabbits here this morning, you know."

"Rabbits?" Judy said. "Really? But where did they come from?"

"Who knows? Maybe they were bombed out too."

"And they found their way here!"

"I bet there are foxes too," Alan added. "There often are in cities. Come early one day and see."

Come early one day and see … Judy thought of dawn in the ruins with Alan. Pale grey early-morning light. Birdsong. Wild rabbits. It sounded like something in a story.

"What are you going to do today?" Judy asked.

"I do want to take some pictures of the old vicarage," Alan said, "but I won't go inside. Then I'm going to keep an eye on those redstarts. I want to see if I can find the nest."

"OK. I'm going to keep digging through the rubble. So far I've only found a few bits and pieces, but there must be lots of Mum's precious things in there. If I can find them, I could give them to her, I thought." Judy scratched the ground with her toe. "What I really want is photographs," she said, not looking at Alan. "All the pictures of me when I was little are gone … Mum and Dad's wedding pictures too. They must be in there somewhere."

Alan nodded. "All right," he said. "Let's go."
And together they walked towards the house.

The sun was out. The air already felt warmer and brighter.

The ginger cat was curled up on the top of a wall, watching them approach.

"Hey, puss-puss-puss," said Judy.

The cat allowed her to stroke it, then jumped off the wall and bounded away.

Judy sat down on a heap of rubble and began to work. She lifted the bricks and piled them neatly to the side. Now and then, she looked at the back of the house. And at the rooms still standing.

It wasn't safe. Not even a little bit. Looters had left this part of the house alone, and so had Judy. It wasn't safe at all. But there were four whole rooms – just *there*. Untouched.

Every time Judy came to the bomb site, she looked at them.

How dangerous would it be to go inside, really?

Chapter 8

The Crypt

Alan was nearly as fascinated with the vicarage as Judy was. He took out his camera and spent a long time circling the house, looking for the best shot. When he was happy, he pressed the button and – *Click! Click!* – took the photograph.

Judy watched him as he worked. Alan frowned, thought, waited. He was completely absorbed in his photography. Judy rather liked it. She liked people who cared about things.

As she watched, Judy began to hear a noise. A sort of buzzing sound, like a helicopter. Far away at first but getting slowly louder.

Alan stiffened.

"What is it?" said Judy. Then, when he didn't move, she said, "Why are you looking like that? What's wrong?"

"It's a buzz-bomb," said Alan.

"A *what?*"

"A doodlebug – oh, you *must* have heard of them! They're like bombs without pilots. They just fly and fly until they then fall out of the sky. We had masses of them drop on London last summer."

"Flying bombs," said Judy. She remembered the lady in the National Restaurant talking about the buzz-bombs now. "Wouldn't there be an air-raid siren?" she said nervously.

"Usually," said Alan. "But sometimes there's only one and it's missed ..."

The noise was still getting louder. The buzz-bomb was coming closer. Judy could feel the hairs on her arms rise. Somehow the idea of one bomb, all on its own in the middle of the day, was more creepy than a full-on air raid.

"What should we do?" Judy said. But Alan wasn't listening. He was looking up at the sky.

"There!" he said.

Judy squinted. There it was. The bomb looked like a squat black beetle, with little wings and a tail. It made a low *put-put-put* sound. And it was getting closer.

"Is it going to land on us?" Judy said.

"I don't know," said Alan. He was frowning. "You can't tell when it's going to drop – that's the trouble. It just cuts out. Then ..." He held up his fist, then opened his fingers. *Boom.*

"Shouldn't we hide or something?" Judy said.

Alan didn't move.

"Alan!" she said more urgently. "What should we do?" Her heart began to speed up. The bomb's engine sounded sputtery and tired. It really felt like it was about to cut out. Surely they should get to a shelter, or a cellar at least? But Judy felt awkward suggesting it when Alan was just standing there.

Would she really rather die than look like a fool?

Alan didn't seem bothered by the bomb at all. "It's still going," he pointed out.

"Even so ..." said Judy. "We could hide in the crypt in the church."

Alan shrugged. Judy hesitated, then made a decision. She set off towards the steps into the crypt. She hadn't been down them since she'd come back to London – the steps didn't look safe at all. But she had seen the entrance in the shell of the church. The old wooden door, half opened.

"What *is* that?" asked Alan behind her.

"It's the crypt," said Judy. "It's where they used to bury people. Important people who gave money to the church."

Alan shuddered.

"It's not scary," said Judy. "Come on."

She set off down the stairs. They were slimy with moss and damp, but the handrail was still there. Judy went slowly and carefully, feeling her way for rubble. Alan followed.

"You've been down here?" he asked.

"Not for years," said Judy. She had a sudden memory of coming down these steps with her father. Holding his hand. The quiet, churchy feeling of the place.

"It's creepy," said Alan.

"No, it isn't," said Judy. She had never been frightened in the church. "It's holy."

They stood just under the roof, where there was still light. The *put-put-put* sound of the buzz-bomb grew louder. Judy felt a bit calmer here, though she knew that if the bomb did fall on the church, they could still be in trouble. People died in direct hits, even when they were hiding underground. Could she and Alan die? Judy knew they could, of course. But it didn't feel real.

"I think it's passed us," said Alan.

"Are you sure?" said Judy. She tried to sound calm, but her heart was fluttering inside her chest.

"It's going over the high street."

"The high street!" Judy's voice came out as a squeak. The high street! Uncle Jack's house. The school! All the shops. All those people.

She listened, trying to make sense of it. *Please don't fall, please don't fall.*

It didn't. The buzz-bomb carried on, the *put-put-put* growing fainter. Judy breathed out.

"There!" she said. "They're safe."

Alan gave her an odd look.

"Well," he said. "It's going to fall *somewhere*."

Judy tried to make sense of that thought, but it was too big for her to hold in her head. The bomb had missed them, but it would hit someone else. Perhaps a park, or an empty house. But probably somewhere there were people. An office. A school. A shop. It was a horrible thought. How could you be glad about that? But she was glad. Glad that it had missed them and the streets that she knew. Glad that they were still alive.

Now it was Judy's turn to shudder. Alan must have noticed.

"Come on," he said. "There's nothing you can do about it. You just have to not think about it."

But how could you not think about something like that?

Chapter 9

The Rubble

After that, Judy and Alan met most days at the bomb site. They settled into a quiet routine. Alan would lie in the grass for hours, watching the birds and the other wildlife. Sometimes he would take photographs, but often he would just be there, looking.

Judy would work away at the ruins. She was finding more things every day. An old book with swollen water-logged pages. Broken china. A leather glove with a hole in the finger. She kept the things she found in an old steam trunk, hidden under some planks. Most of it was junk – she knew that. But she kept digging.

Judy and Alan both brought sandwiches, and every day they ate their lunch together.

"A lunch break!" said Judy. She thought this was funny. Like they were workmen or something. But Alan didn't laugh.

"That's right," he said. Judy felt ashamed, though she didn't really understand why.

Every day they came, there was more life. More green. There was more birdsong. Alan pointed out a blackbird's nest in one of the trees and rabbit holes in the graveyard. He was always noticing things.

"It's because I stay still," he said to Judy. "You're always moving about."

"I'm doing things!" said Judy, rather crossly. "There's nothing wrong with doing!"

Alan shrugged.

"If you want to see things, you have to know how to wait," he said.

It was hard for Judy to know what Alan was thinking – was he pleased to see her? Did he like her? She supposed he must, or he wouldn't come every day. But he gave very little away. Judy's friends from the grammar school in Somerset had always been shrieking and laughing and telling each other what they thought. They wrote her long gushing letters now about how much they missed her. But Alan didn't tell her what he was thinking, so she had to look for other clues. Like the way he saved up new discoveries in the churchyard to show Judy. "Look, owl pellets!" he'd say. "Look, caterpillars!"

"Look, celandines!" Alan said today.

"I know celandines," Judy said. "There was a whole bank of them in the woods behind our house in Somerset."

"Lucky you," said Alan.

Judy nodded. "I loved it," she said.

They stood there in silence for a moment, not saying anything. But Judy felt sure that Alan understood all the things she wasn't saying out loud: how strange it was to be back and how guilty she felt about missing the aunties when she should have been happy to be with Mum again.

"I'm going to have a wood behind my house one day," Alan said suddenly. Judy felt like he'd given her a gift. It was so rare for Alan to talk about himself like that.

One day, Alan didn't come at all, but the next day he was back again as usual. He didn't say why he hadn't been there yesterday, and Judy didn't ask. Every time she tried to talk about Alan's family, or his life outside of the bomb site, he changed the subject. The message was clear: this was private. Judy took the hint.

"Look what I've got," he said when they were eating lunch. He rummaged in his satchel and pulled out a paper bag.

"What is it?" she said. Then added, "Oh! Photographs!"

They were good. There was one of the church tower rising up from the ruin, all covered in ivy. Another of the broken windows with the sun streaming through them. One of the house. One of a blackbird sitting on a tombstone. One of a rabbit.

Judy's favourite photograph was of the ruined vicarage. It showed the grass stalks poking out of the rubble, with the house behind it. At the front was Judy herself, sitting on one of the fallen beams. She had a streak of mud across her forehead and she was wearing her gardening gloves. She looked … at home. Happy.

"You're rather good at photography, aren't you?" she said. She meant it.

Alan looked a bit awkward and a bit pleased. "You can keep it if you want," he said.

"Really?" Judy asked.

He nodded.

She took it happily. Alan stood up. "Photographs are for looking at," he said. "There's no point me just keeping it in a drawer."

Then, looking rather embarrassed, he bit into his sandwich.

There was a letter waiting for Judy on Saturday morning. It was sitting on the hall table when she went into Uncle Jack's house to clean her teeth.

It was a sunny day. She sat on the back step and opened the envelope. The letter was from Auntie Poll and Auntie Betty:

Dear Judy,

We hope you are well and your mum is well and you are enjoying London. Have you started school yet? Tell your mum you can always come back here if the schools don't open. Next-door's cat had three grey kittens. We are going to have one. Jimmy Williams fell into the duckpond and cut his leg on an old bedstead, but he is all right now. A blackbird has built a nest in the hawthorn.

We thought maybe you could come and stay for a week in the summer and give your mum a break. You know your room is always there waiting for you.

Love from
Auntie Poll and Auntie Betty

Judy tipped up the envelope. A little dried flower fell out. A bluebell.

Judy stared at it. She felt very strange.

She wondered what her mum would say about Judy going back to Somerset for a holiday. She liked London and she liked her mum. But all of a sudden Judy missed her little room under the eaves so much it was like a pain.

"Judy!"

She looked up.

"Dad!"

There he was in his chaplain's uniform. He looked the same as he always did, with his thinning hair and his bald spot and his little Charlie Chaplin moustache and the wrinkles round his eyes. Her dad's hair was a bit greyer than the last time she'd seen him. But his smile was just the same.

Judy jumped up, dropping the letter onto the floor, and ran into his arms. He lifted her up off the ground and spun her around. He smelt of Dad: boot-polish and peppermints and air-force uniform.

Then Mum was there, running down the caravan steps with her hair still in its curlers. And Dad was hugging Mum so tightly that they looked like one person. Judy felt suddenly embarrassed, like she was spying on something private. But then Dad looked up and saw her watching. Mum and Dad pulled apart.

"I got away early," he said. He looked at Judy. "You've grown!"

Then, "What shall we do?" he said.

It was a nearly perfect day. First, they went to Kew Gardens and looked all around. Judy liked looking at the flowers, but the gardens felt rather tame and formal compared to the bomb site. Then they went and had tea and chocolate cake in a Lyons tearoom.

"This is as good as the cake I had for my birthday!" Judy said without thinking. She saw Mum's smile vanish, and she immediately regretted saying anything. But Dad smiled.

"I suppose there's more food in the countryside," he said.

"Well, yes," Judy said. "Auntie Poll and Auntie Betty had chickens. And they used to do mending for Mr Wilson, and he'd give them butter in return. They made cake for all my birthdays."

"All right for some," said Mum with a sniff.

Dad said gently, "How kind of them. I'm so glad you lived with good people."

Judy looked at him gratefully.

"They said we could visit whenever we wanted," she said. "They only have one spare bedroom, but you can rent rooms in the Royal Oak. That's the pub in town."

Mum made a huffing sort of noise. Judy tried not to show that she minded. But she did. The Blitz wasn't Auntie Betty and Auntie Poll's fault. Couldn't Mum just be pleased that Judy had been happy?

They talked about other things while they finished eating the cake. But when Mum went up to pay, Dad said to Judy, "Maybe we could go and

74

visit your aunties, you and I. I don't think it'll be long until my unit is disbanded."

"I'd like that," said Judy. She wondered if she could ask her dad about going to stay with them in the summer. She was still a bit shy around her dad. She didn't know him as well as her mum.

"They said I could stay for a week on my own if I wanted to," Judy said.

"And do you want to?" Dad asked.

"Yes, of course." Judy was surprised. How could he even ask? "I haven't told Mum," she said. "I wasn't sure …"

Dad sighed. "It's not been easy for your mum," he said.

"I know," Judy said quickly. She *did* know that. She was always being careful about how Mum felt. Why was nobody careful about her?

"I'll talk to her," Dad promised. "I'm sure it'll be all right."

The hard, sad place in her stomach relaxed a little. It had been so awful to think that she might never go back to Somerset again. Judy hadn't realised how awful until Dad had said that.

For dinner, they had fish and chips with hot cups of tea, and then they went to the pictures. They saw a newsreel, a Mickey Mouse cartoon and a very silly film about an earl who fell in love with a parlour maid. Judy loved it.

"Happy?" said Dad as they walked home, and Judy sighed.

"It's been *wonderful*."

It was nice going to bed knowing that Dad would be there when Judy woke up. She had to give up her double bed to Mum and Dad, and sleep on the bunk, but Judy didn't even mind that. The caravan felt smaller with him there, but in a nice way. Cosier. She closed her eyes and drifted off to sleep ...

"No! No, get me out! Get me out!"

Judy woke up with a gasp. It was still dark. Someone was shouting. It was her mum.

"No! No!" Mum shouted.

"What's happening?" said Judy.

Someone – Dad? – turned the torch on in the double bed. Judy could hear him talking softly behind the curtains.

"Shhh ... hush, darling. You're safe."

The caravan was cold. Judy pulled on her dressing gown and went over to the double bed. Mum was sitting up and crying. Dad had his arms around her.

Chapter 10

Uncle Jack's House

At breakfast, Mum was her normal bright, cheerful self. Clearly she didn't want to talk about last night. Dad and Judy said nothing. They went to church as usual.

After church, they had Sunday lunch with Uncle Jack in the big dark dining room. Judy hated it. They sat around the dining table, eating dry boiled beef and stewed apples. Uncle Jack had a housekeeper who did all his cooking and cleaning for him. He had wanted Mum to come and do it after she was bombed out. But Mum had said no.

Mum was almost always cheerful. But her cheerfulness was different in Uncle Jack's house. It flickered in and out like a candle.

"Is that child still out of school?" Uncle Jack said, looking at Judy.

"That's right," said Judy's mum. Flicker-flicker went her smile. "The grammar school isn't back yet. I think a lot of the girls are still in the countryside."

Uncle Jack made a noise that sounded like "Harrumph!"

"Never saw the point of grammar schools," he said. He glared at Dad. "When are you coming home then? Can't have your wife and kid squatting in my garden for ever, eh?"

"As soon as the air force release me, I'll be back," Dad said calmly. "I don't think it'll be long. They aren't flying raids any more. We're very grateful for all your help."

"Eh. Well," Uncle Jack said. He didn't look pleased. "Least I could do, eh?"

Judy frowned. Sometimes she hated living in Uncle Jack's back yard.

Dad was clearly thinking the same thing. Once they were back in the caravan, he said, "I wish you two didn't have to live here. Are you sure you couldn't find somewhere else?"

"Where?" said Mum. "There's a national housing shortage."

"There must be somewhere," said Dad.

"I like our caravan," said Mum. "It's like being a Girl Guide again. If we had a horse, we could go touring the country. We could go to the seaside! Wouldn't that be useful, with all the petrol shortages?"

Judy giggled. Dad frowned. Mum stuck her tongue out at him. "We have fun here, don't we, Judy?"

"Yes," said Judy. She did like the caravan.

"But wouldn't you like your own bedroom?" said Dad. "Somewhere to put all your things?"

"I suppose so," Judy replied. Of course she wanted her own bedroom. And a proper living room, with proper armchairs. Space for her books. But she *did* like the caravan too. And she felt like she should be on Mum's side on this. It was Mum who lived here, after all, not Dad. She felt like Mum should be the one who got to choose where her home was – at least until Dad came back. "We're not going to be here for ever though, are we?" Judy said.

"Certainly not!" said Dad.

"I might stay here," said Mum. "Saves me having to clean so much." And she stuck her tongue out again.

*

Dad went back to the air-force base the next morning. When he said goodbye to Judy, he said, "Look after Mum!"

"Of course," said Judy.

"That's my girl," said Dad. Then he hugged her so tightly that she thought he'd never let go.

Chapter 11

The Living Room

After Dad had gone, Judy felt a little flat. Mum had Monday morning off from the National Restaurant because of Dad being here, so she and Judy had lunch together, sitting on the caravan steps.

"Nice to be able to sit outside, isn't it?" said Mum. She stretched out her arms and smiled. "It's been a long winter."

After lunch, Judy set off for the bomb site. She wondered if Alan had missed her. Would he say anything about her not being there?

He was lying on his favourite tombstone, his binoculars pointing at the hedgerow.

"Hello!" said Judy.

Alan grunted.

"My dad had leave!" Judy said, sitting on the tombstone beside him. She was determined not to let Alan's silence bother her. "He's a chaplain – in the air force. He was home for two whole days!"

Another grunt. Alan was scowling.

"Is *your* dad in the forces?" Judy asked.

"No," said Alan abruptly.

Clearly he didn't want to talk about fathers. Judy wondered why. Maybe his father was dead. People's fathers did die, in the Blitz and the war. She wondered if she dared ask him but decided not to. Alan didn't seem in the mood to talk.

Judy wandered over to the vicarage and sat looking at it. She was beginning to get rather frustrated with the rubble heap. Alan was right – it had been well picked over by boys looking for pieces of bombs and looters looking for valuables. What was left was water-logged and broken. This was rather depressing.

Judy had been so excited when she'd found a blue cardigan trapped under an armchair. She *remembered* that cardigan. Her mum had knitted it herself. It was thick and chunky and Mum used to wear it on cold evenings, sitting by the fire. Judy wanted to take it home and show it to her mum. Maybe they could wash it and Mum could wear it again? But when Judy had dug out the rest, she had seen it would be no use. The cardigan was filthy and torn in several places. It had begun to rot away. It wasn't anything special any more. It was rubbish.

Judy had been more upset by this than she'd felt like she should be. It was just a cardigan. Mum had probably forgotten all about it. But that cardigan was one of the few things she could really remember about living at home. She hated that it had been spoilt.

Today Judy couldn't stop thinking about the rest of the vicarage, the part that was still standing. If she looked through Alan's binoculars, she could see all sorts of things in there. A whole bookcase full of books. Cupboards full of clothes and toys.

She went closer. There was the kitchen with the yellow cupboards, and the wooden table still lying there on the floor. *Had* looters been inside the house? There were wooden spoons still hanging from the rack on the wall. But surely some things were missing? Hadn't there been a picture on that back wall?

Judy was almost at the ruin now, closer than she had ever been before. Her heart was thudding in her chest. Why was she so nervous?

The house looked much more solid close up than it did from the other side of the rubble. Ivy was growing up the walls, which were leaning at a wild angle. But they were thick and sturdy. Perhaps if she didn't touch them, she'd be all right ...

Judy looked at the kitchen. One more step and she'd be inside. In the house she'd lived in with her mother and father.

Perhaps if Judy went inside, it would stop mattering so much to her. She would stop minding about her old life and find a way to be happy with what she had now.

She clambered over the fallen bricks to the edge of the living room. This room was in a poor condition. The sofa and the armchairs were thick with plaster dust and were clearly beginning to rot. The wallpaper was peeling off the walls. But there were still a lot of things untouched. A bookcase full of books, tipped over onto its face. A table with feet like a lion, lying on its side.

And ...

Judy caught her breath.

It was in the pile of books beside the bookcase. A photograph album. A big old black one. It was her mum's. Judy could remember Mum sitting by the fire, sticking photographs into it. She remembered the photographs too. There was Mum and Dad on their wedding day. Judy in a pram with a silver teething ring. Judy with Granny – Granny, who had died when Judy was six.

A photograph album. It was the perfect thing.

Surely it wouldn't be too dangerous to go and get it?

Judy put one foot onto the floor. And then the other foot. She was holding her breath. She mustn't touch the walls. But if she just walked carefully and quietly across the floor – that would be all right, surely?

She took another step. It felt so strange to be in here. Actually *in* her old house. But in a funny way, what was strangest was how much it *wasn't* her house. It was filthy and mouldy and smelt of something rotten. There were mushrooms growing on the back of the sofa. Judy had thought being in here would feel amazing, but it didn't. It was a dead place. It wasn't a home any more.

She took another careful step. The floor creaked underneath her. Was the wood rotten? Judy hadn't thought of that. She put a hand on the back of the sofa to steady herself. She was halfway across the room now. She couldn't go back yet.

Another step. And another. The smell was stronger. And now here she was by the books. The floor was covered in broken glass where the glass doors of the bookcase had smashed. Judy looked at the books spread across the floor, but there were none that she recognised. They were all grown-up books – hardbacks in dull cloth bindings. They looked very serious.

The photograph album was halfway down the pile. Judy lifted the other books off the top, then picked up the album. It was damp and swollen, but it was still in one piece. It was protected a little by the top floor of the house, of course.

Judy stood up. She should look for other things to take with her perhaps, but she found she didn't want to. This place didn't belong to her any more. She just wanted to get out as fast as she could.

She turned to come back and stopped. Alan was there, standing on the edge of the rubble.

"What are you doing?" he said. He sounded angry.

"I'm coming back!" Judy said. She tried not to speak too loudly. The leaning walls looked more alarming now she was underneath them. If the roof fell in, Judy would die. She knew that with absolute certainty. Perhaps it had been a stupid thing to do, to come in here. She took another step forward.

"Come back at once!" said Alan. He *was* angry. "You could be killed!"

"I am," Judy said. Maybe he couldn't hear her? The floor creaked under her again.

She looked up quickly at Alan and caught his eye. He looked worried.

"Just come slowly," he said. "Slowly and carefully. For God's sake!"

"It's fine," Judy said. "It's just—"

And then, with a horrible, splintering crash, the floor gave way beneath her feet.

Chapter 12

The Wreckage

It all happened so fast. Judy crashed down through the floorboards and into the foundations of the house. She landed with a sickening thump. The whole house seemed to be shaking. *Oh God. Oh God.* It was going to topple down onto her head. She was going to be crushed. *Oh God, please save me*, she prayed. *Oh God, I'm sorry. Oh God ...*

Judy cowered in the hole, waiting as the house trembled around her. She was standing in a jagged hole in the floorboards. Her legs were in the foundations, under the floor; her top half was above it. There was a sickening rumble. She squeezed her eyes closed. And then ...

Silence.

She opened her eyes. The house was still standing. But ... *oh God* ... it had shifted slightly.

It was now leaning even more dangerously to the side.

"Judy! Judy! Are you all right?" Alan called.

He was clambering over the rubble towards her. His face looked white.

"I'm fine!" Judy said. "At least ..." She tried to move and gasped. Her legs hurt. She must have cut them when she fell through the floor. "I've cut my legs a bit. But I don't think they're badly hurt."

"I told you not to go in there," said Alan. He looked frightened. He came closer. "Can you get yourself out? Or do you need help?"

"I don't know." Judy tried to pull herself up and gasped. "Ow!"

"I'm going to get help," said Alan. "Don't move, OK?"

"All right," said Judy. She watched as he climbed back over the rubble. *Please be quick*, she thought. But she didn't say it out loud.

It felt very strange to be here all alone. Judy stayed as still as she could, but she couldn't stop looking at the walls of the house. The longer she looked at them, the more precarious they seemed, like something in a trick photograph. They *must* fall, mustn't they? And there was a whole other floor and a roof above her head. If they landed on top of Judy, she would die.

Oh, please, God, I don't want to die, she prayed. The church said God loved you, but he didn't always save you. She knew that from her father.

Judy closed her eyes. But it was worse not being able to see. She opened them quickly again.

How long Alan was taking. Where had he gone to find help anyway?

Why didn't they come?

And then, suddenly, she thought, *How long did Mum have to wait in the darkness?* That must have been worse than this. At least Judy was outside in the sunshine. At least she knew someone was coming. *How long had Mum waited there alone?*

At last, after what felt like years, Judy saw them. Three men clambering over the bomb site with Alan. Were they firemen or air-raid wardens? Firemen, she decided. Those weren't air-raid uniforms.

Judy waved but didn't call out. She was growing more nervous the longer she waited here.

They waved back to her. Then there was another wait. They stood in a little huddle, talking to each other. At last, two of the men came over to the edge of the bomb site.

"We're going to put some supports on the house," one of them said. "It's going to take a while, I'm afraid. But we can't come and get you when it's leaning like this. Are you all right? Are you hurt?"

"Something's wrong with my legs," Judy called. "I think I hurt them when I fell through the floor. They're all right if I don't move."

Actually, they were starting to hurt more now. She'd hardly noticed them at first. But now there was a sort of dull throbbing ache all along her legs.

"All right," said the fireman. He sounded worried. "Do your parents have a telephone?"

"No," said Judy. Uncle Jack did, but she didn't know the number. She told the fireman where the National Restaurant was, and he nodded and gave her a thumbs up.

"I'll go," said Alan. He looked pleased to have a job to do.

There was more waiting. Judy was beginning to get cold. Then, at long, long last, more men appeared with long wooden props, which they began to fit around the house. But where was Mum? Why wasn't she coming?

And then suddenly there she was. Mum was hurrying across the bomb site with Alan. She hadn't even put on her hat. Judy felt a sudden rush of love at the sight of her.

"Judy!" Mum cried as she came closer. "Judy, my darling! What on earth were you thinking?"

And then Judy was crying too.

It was dark by the time the firemen reached Judy, and Alan had had to go home. They waited until the props were in place, then they wriggled across the wooden floor on their stomachs. Judy was tired of standing in the same position in the hole, and cold. She couldn't stop shivering. Her legs were really hurting now. But once the men reached her it was all very fast. They lifted her out and laid her on a stretcher, Judy still clutching the photograph album.

"I don't need a stretcher!" she said, but they did it anyway. And it was so nice to be looked after that she didn't complain. They slid Judy across the floor, and then Mum was there and she was holding

Judy. She knew then that everything was going to be all right.

"Oh, my girl!" Mum cried. "What were you doing *there*?"

And suddenly Judy was crying again.

"I just wanted to see what it was like ..." Judy said.

"But, my darling," said Mum. "It's not our house any more. It's just a ruin. There's nothing left ..."

And Judy cried and cried. Because Mum was right. There *was* nothing left.

"You lost everything ..." Judy sobbed. "You and Dad. All your things. Didn't you mind? I thought ... I wanted to get them back ... but ..."

And then Mum was crying too.

"I don't care about any of that," she said. "Books and photographs – they're just bits of paper. Tables and chairs – they're only wood. If anything had happened to you ... my girl ... my darling girl ..."

Chapter 13

A New Place

The ambulance took Judy and her mother to the hospital.

"I don't need an ambulance," Judy said. "I'm fine, really." But she couldn't stop shaking, and the lady in the ambulance didn't listen.

At the hospital, a nurse gave her hot, sweet tea and wrapped her in a blanket. A doctor came and looked at Judy's legs.

"Nothing's broken," he said. "But you've cut them up quite badly. You'll need stitches. And you'll need to stay at home and rest."

Mum held Judy's hand while the doctor stitched her wounds. And afterwards Mum insisted on paying for a taxi to take them home.

In the caravan, Mum lit the stove and heated up a tin of tomato soup. Judy sat in bed and drank it. It was lovely. Like being warmed up from the inside. Her mum sat on the bench and watched her without saying anything. *Are we just not going to talk about this?* Judy wondered.

She had given her mum the photograph album. Mum had just put it in her bag without looking at it. Didn't it matter to her at all?

"I found a lot of things in the house," Judy said suddenly.

Mum didn't answer.

"There's that photograph album," said Judy. "But there are other things too. Just little things. A love spoon. Some books. I was going to give them to you. But I wanted to keep them for a bit first. I wanted to remember what it was like to have a home."

"Was it so awful, being evacuated?" said Mum.

Awful! How could Mum think such a thing? For a moment, Judy was angry, but she tried not to show it. After all, this was the first time Mum had tried to talk to her about being evacuated. Judy should answer her properly.

"No," Judy said. "It wasn't, not really. Auntie Poll and Auntie Betty were very kind to me. But ..." She hesitated. "It wasn't a home. Not a real one."

"No," said Mum. "No, it wouldn't have been. I am sorry, you know. I would never have chosen to send you away. You do know that, don't you?"

"Of course," said Judy. She had always known that.

They sat for a while without saying anything.

"Was it very awful for you?" Judy said. "I mean, when Dad and I went away?"

Mum sighed. "You make the best of it," she said. "So many people have worse things to worry about. But I'll never forgive Hitler for stealing your childhood from me."

Her voice was quiet, but there was real anger in it. Judy didn't know how to answer.

"I missed you too," Judy said. It was a rather flat little sentence for how much she *had* missed Mum and Dad. But she didn't know how to put that loneliness into words. Just thinking about it made Judy feel stiff and shy all over. "And I miss Auntie Poll and Auntie Betty. Mum, I can love you and Dad and I can love them too. I can be glad to be home and sorry that I'm not there in Somerset at the same time. That's a good thing, isn't it? That I was happy there and happy here too?"

"I suppose it is," said Mum. She smiled at Judy. "Goodness me. When did you get so wise?"

Judy didn't think she was wise. She thought what she'd said was obvious. But maybe Mum couldn't see that.

"You can't blame me if I'm jealous sometimes," Mum went on. "Your aunties got five years of my lovely girl and I had no one."

"You've got me now," said Judy. She put her cup of soup down on the table and wrapped her arms around Mum. "I'm not going anywhere again. I promise."

Mum kissed her. Judy wondered if Mum was always going to need looking after a bit. How strange. Part of her liked it, being the adult one. But quite a lot of her missed the days when her mother was the one who always knew what to do and say to make things better. Was that what happened when you grew up? Your mother stopped being all-powerful and turned into a human being? Was it a good thing or a bad one? You lost something, but maybe you got something else in return.

"Was it awful, being trapped?" Judy said. "When our house was bombed, I mean."

Mum didn't reply for a long moment. Then, at last, she said, "Yes. For a long time afterwards, every time I went in a house, I got panicky. I kept thinking about what would happen if a stray plane came over while I was inside."

"Oh." Judy was quiet. "Is that why you like the caravan?" she asked.

"Yes," Mum said. "Silly, isn't it? I know the war is nearly over, but ... it doesn't feel over. We still get buzz-bombs sometimes. Hitler hasn't gone away. The caravan just feels safer. But your dad's right – we can't stay here for ever. Not when he comes home. There won't be room."

"We could run away and join the circus," said Judy.

Mum laughed. "No," she said. "You need to go to school. And also ..." Mum paused. She seemed to be trying to find the right words. "Sometimes you need to stop hiding. I love London. Your dad loves being a vicar here. I need to find a way to make that work for us all."

"Dad said sometimes things only come out when you feel safe," said Judy.

Mum looked surprised. "I don't know about that!" she said. She pushed her hair out of her eyes. "I can't really remember the last time I felt safe," she said.

They were quiet.

"Did you really not mind losing all your things?" asked Judy.

"Did you mind leaving your toys behind when you went to the countryside?" asked Mum.

Judy tried to remember.

"No," she said. "Not really. I just missed you and Dad."

Mum nodded. "You and your dad back home," she said. "It's all I wanted. I can cope with anything if I have you two."

The next day, Mum insisted Judy stayed at home. Mum didn't go into work either.

"I told them I needed some time off to look after my daughter," she said. "I should have done this weeks ago! I can't think why I didn't."

They played cards, and Judy read her book, and Mum spring-cleaned the caravan. It was a bit nice and a bit strange.

"I should go and tell Alan I'm all right," said Judy.

"You're not going near that bomb site again!" said Mum. "It's too dangerous!"

"But I have to," said Judy. "I have to show you the things I found."

On Saturday, Judy took Mum back to the ruins. The closer they got, the quieter Mum got. Her face looked closed in and tense again.

"Are you all right?" Judy asked. Mum's face tightened.

"Let's get this over with," she said.

"It's not a sad place," said Judy. It felt important that Mum knew this. "Look at the flowers! And the birds! And the angel, watching over us. There's so much life here."

"Maybe," said Mum. But she didn't sound sure. Judy wondered about showing her Alan's photograph of the grass growing through the ruins. But she decided to wait. Perhaps she could show it to Dad. Judy was certain he'd be interested.

Judy took Mum's hand and led her over to the ruined vicarage. She sat down on a beam next to the trunk. "Look what I found," she said, opening the lid. "Old plates! Books! And some toys and things – see."

Mum looked a little wary. But she took the woolly panda and held it in her lap. "Your auntie Mary gave you that for your third birthday," she said.

"Did she?" said Judy.

Mum stroked the panda's grubby ear. She took in a long, shuddering breath.

"Do you want to see the other things?" Judy said. "We can stop if you want."

"No," said Mum. "Let's do this."

So they sat there together in the rubble and looked through the trunk.

Later that evening, Mum was making dinner when she said, "I had a letter from Dad."

Judy looked up from her book. Letters from Dad were an event.

"His squadron is being disbanded," said Mum. "He thought it wouldn't be long."

"You mean Dad's coming home?" said Judy. She could feel something bubbling up inside her. Dad, here! Dad, home! Judy looked around the caravan. "But ... where will we live? Will he come here?"

"Well ..." Mum put the letter down. "There are so many churches without vicars right now. So many young men have joined up. Your dad spoke to his old bishop, and he thinks he's found a new job."

"A new job! As a vicar?" Judy asked.

"That's right," Mum said. "About half an hour away from here. There's a vicarage."

"A real house," said Judy.

"Yes."

"A real home! With Dad!"

"Yes!" Mum said.

They looked at each other. Judy could feel her smile getting wider and wider. Mum was smiling too.

"Do you think there's a grammar school nearby?" said Judy. "And will we need furniture? Do vicarages come with furniture? And bedsheets and things like that?"

"I expect the parish will help us out," said Mum. "They usually do. Heavens, we'll need a lot of things! Pots and pans, plates ..."

"Rubbish bins, coat hangers ..." said Judy happily. A whole house full of ordinary things! It sounded wonderful.

"Wait a moment!" said Mum. "I should get a pen ... make a list ..."

They bent their heads over the piece of paper, talking excitedly.

On Monday, Mum went back to work.

"Are you sure you'll be all right on your own?" she asked Judy.

"I'll be fine," said Judy. "Honestly." And she was. Her legs still hurt a bit if she moved them the wrong way, but they weren't too bad. She could walk about fine.

"And stay away from the bomb site!" said Mum.

"All right," said Judy, but she went anyway.

It wasn't the same though. The bomb site had suddenly become a place people were interested in. It was surrounded by people pointing and whispering. There were new, bigger signs saying DANGER and men working among the ruins, trying to make it safe. It didn't feel like Judy's place any more. She looked for Alan, but she couldn't see him. She knew he wouldn't be there when so many people were around.

After that, Judy stayed away from the bomb site. There was a whole week of glorious sunshine, and she started taking a book and reading it in the park behind the National Restaurant. Mum would come out and join Judy on her breaks, and Judy would go and eat her lunch with the women who worked there. It was nice. Friendly.

Judy liked her mother. She liked finding out about the person she was, this woman who had lost everything and carried on anyway. Judy liked how hard Mum worked and how she always found things to be cheerful about. She wondered why she had ever thought she needed to hide from her. Judy showed her mum the letters from the aunties and told her about her friends at the grammar school in Somerset – Margaret and Lillian and Joan. Mum said she'd like to meet them.

"Dad said we could go back in the summer maybe," said Judy.

Mum looked a bit surprised. "All right," she said. Then she smiled. "I think we all deserve a holiday."

On Friday, Judy went back to the little library to change her books.

"Haven't seen you in a while," the librarian said.

"No," said Judy.

"Well," said the librarian. She smiled at Judy. "Enjoy the sunshine!"

Judy took her books and walked down the high street. She had only been away a week or so, but already everything looked different. There were flowers growing in the window boxes. Weeds sprouting from the cracks in the school playground. A mother and two little girls were buying ice lollies from a corner shop. Children really were coming back to London again. Judy went into the shop and bought an ice cream cone. She ate it slowly, walking down the street.

When Judy got to the bomb site, she stopped. It looked quiet today. The DANGER notices were still there, but the men working on the ruin were gone. There was nobody there except a tramp feeding biscuits to a scrappy little terrier. The dog barked and the tramp put his hand on his collar.

"Now then, lad," he said to the dog. "She won't hurt you!"

Judy smiled at the tramp. She had been nervous of tramps when she'd first come back to London. But today this man didn't seem frightening.

"Good morning!" Judy said.

"And a very good morning to you too," said the tramp.

She picked her way through the long grass. Like the high street, everything here seemed to have changed just in the short time she'd been away. Judy could smell the sweet, heavy smell of spring. There were dandelions in the long grass, blossom on the trees above her head.

She walked through the graveyard. And there Alan was, as she had known he would be. He lay on his stomach on a tombstone, pointing his binoculars into the bushes. Judy stopped, watching him. She knew so little about him, she realised. Who were his family? Where *was* his father – was he dead? Why did he hate the grammar school so much? Why was he so desperate to get back to the countryside? Alan kept so much of himself private. It would take a long time before he trusted her enough to show her those secret places in himself, she thought. But it would be worth the effort when he did.

Judy took another step forward.

Alan lowered his binoculars.

"I can hear you, you know," he said, without turning around. "Didn't anyone ever tell you not to step on twigs?"

Author spotlight

Sally Nicholls was born in Stockton, just after midnight, in a thunderstorm. She's always loved stories and spent her childhood trying to make real life work like it does in books. At the age of twenty-two she enrolled on an MA in Writing for Young People at the University of Bath Spa, where she wrote her first novel, *Ways to Live Forever*.

Sally has published nearly twenty books for children and teenagers. She has won many awards, including the Waterstones Children's Book Prize. Her YA novel about the suffrage movement, *Things a Bright Girl Can Do*, was shortlisted for the Carnegie Medal, and *An Island of Our Own* was shortlisted for the Costa Book of the Year and the Guardian Children's Book Prize. Her books have been translated into over twenty languages, and *Ways to Live Forever* was made into a feature film. Sally lives in Liverpool with her husband and two children.

Background to the novel

Second World War

Out of the Rubble is set in 1945, towards the end of the five and a half years of the Second World War (which lasted from 1939 to 1945). Countries from all around the world were involved in or affected by the war. The Axis Powers (the name given to Germany, Italy and Japan) fought against the Allies (the name given to the countries that fought the Axis Powers and which included France, Great Britain, the United States and the Soviet Union). People from across the British Commonwealth went to fight or help in countries all around the world: in the story, Judy's friends' dads are in Africa, Europe or Japan. By February 1945, when Judy arrives home in London, the Allies are winning the war in Europe. Many people died during the war including an estimated 15 million soldiers in combat worldwide and 70,000 civilians from Britain alone. British civilians were mostly killed during air raids. Judy's mum nearly died in a bomb attack, and Judy guesses that Alan's father is dead because "People's fathers did die, in the Blitz and the war".

The Blitz

The Blitz was a German bombing campaign against the United Kingdom in 1940 and 1941. The German air force dropped bombs on London and other cities for nine months. It was called the Blitz after the German word *blitzkrieg*, which means "lightning war". People ran to and regularly slept in shelters for safety during the attacks. Judy's mum hid in the cellar at home, and Alan and his family slept in the London Underground. In just one night, the bombs killed nearly 1,500 people in London, and destroyed 11,000 homes. Lots of buildings were left in ruins until after the war had ended, when rebuilding could begin.

Evacuation

Near the start of the Second World War, the government set up an evacuation plan so that school children, like Judy and Alan, and other vulnerable people could leave the big cities in case of bomb or gas attacks. Parents could choose whether they evacuated their children, but many felt they had no choice but to send them to safer areas. Judy was sent to Somerset and Alan was sent to the New Forest. Evacuees were looked after by strangers or relatives who took them into their homes. Judy was looked after by two women who weren't relatives but were kind to her. Alan lived with a man who was a birdwatcher. Some evacuees (like Judy and Alan) enjoyed their countryside life, but others were homesick or lived with people who made them unhappy. Parents missed their children and a few, like Alan's mum, asked for their children to come home to the cities, despite the danger of air raids.

Rationing

During the Second World War, there were also food shortages in Britain. It was difficult to make food because factories had been bombed, and many food-factory workers and farmers were away fighting. It was also difficult to import food from other countries because transport networks were unsafe and ships were attacked. To share the food that was available equally, the government gave households ration books that contained vouchers. At shops, people paid for their food but also had to give in a voucher. The vouchers were for foods that there were limited amounts of, such as tea, cheese, meat and jam. People in the countryside could get some foods more easily because there were cows for milk and butter, pigs for bacon and chickens for eggs. A person in London would have vouchers for just one egg a week, but in the countryside, if you kept chickens, you would have more eggs without needing vouchers. Judy takes butter and eggs home to London from the countryside because, as Auntie Poll says, "There's never as much food in cities."

Men and women

Before the war, it was mostly women who would look after the homes and families, while men went out to work. However, when the war began, men were expected to leave their homes to join the armed forces and, usually, fight. Many went off to war and never came back. Women had to take up much of their work, as well as continue to look after the home. From 1941, the government asked women aged 18 to 60 to choose a job to help the war effort. By the middle of 1943, around 80 per cent of women were employed: working in food production on farms, in factories or in the armed forces. In cities like London, many women helped Blitz victims or the poor and hungry, just as Judy's mum did by working in the National Restaurant.

Who's who in the novel?

Judy is fourteen years old when she returns home to London after living for five years in the country as an evacuee. In London, Judy doesn't feel at home or close to her mum. She explores the vicarage where she lived before the war, which is now in ruins because it was bombed in the Blitz. In the rubble, she hopes to find memories of her past.

Judy's mum lives in a caravan and works at the National Restaurant. She was buried in the cellar when the family home was hit by a bomb. She won't talk about her experience and is upset when Judy talks about happy times as an evacuee.

Judy's dad is away in Brighton where he has a wartime job as the air-force chaplain. He comes home for a few days' leave and explains how Judy's mum keeps problems locked away inside herself.

Uncle Jack volunteers as an air-raid warden. He let Judy's mum set up home in a caravan in the back yard of his "big, cold, dark" house. But he is always cross about her living there, and grumpy that Judy isn't going to school.

Alan is fourteen years old. When he is looking at wildlife in the graveyard, he meets Judy, who is looking at her home that has been ruined by the bombs. He hasn't told his family that he has left school and wants to work with animals instead of going to university. He won't talk about his father and seems happier alone, but still becomes friends with Judy.

Auntie Poll and Auntie Betty are two kind old ladies (not real aunts) who look after Judy in their basic Somerset cottage for five years, while she is an evacuee. Judy finds it exciting to live with oil lamps and candles for light and have chickens and a garden. In London, Judy misses her kind aunts and their country life.

What to read next

Carrie's War by Nina Bawden

A mystery story about Carrie, who returns to the countryside where she had been an evacuee for many years during the Second World War. We slowly discover through flashbacks that Carrie did something as an evacuee that she can't let go.

Edgar & Adolf by Phil Earle and Michael Wagg

The story of Adi and his mission to track down Edgar Kail and return to him a prized possession. His quest becomes a journey of discovery as he learns of a friendship that survived decades, a great football rivalry, and a war that shook the world.

Back Home by Michelle Magorian

Twelve-year-old Rusty was evacuated to the United States and must adapt to a bleak Britain of rules and rationing when she returns home. But it's hard when her mother seems like a stranger, she has a new brother and she must attend a strict boarding school. So Rusty finds a like-minded friend and rebels.

What do you think?

1. At first, Judy finds coming home to London strange. What do you think she finds strange?

2. Do you think Judy misses the home in Somerset where she stayed as an evacuee? Why?

3. Think about the relationship between Judy and her mum. How does it change during the story?

4. How do you feel about Uncle Jack? Why do you think he behaves the way he does?

5. Neither Judy's mum nor Alan want to talk to Judy about the bombing or the Blitz. Why do you think this is?

6. Judy wants to look for things in the rubble of her old family home. What is she hoping to find?

7. In what ways do you think Alan and Judy are similar, and in what ways are they different?

Quick quiz

When you have finished reading *Out of the Rubble*, answer these questions to see how much you can remember about the novel. The answers are on page 123.

1. What county was Judy evacuated to?

2. Who did Judy stay with for five years as an evacuee?

3. What did Judy bring home to London in a basket?

4. Whose house is Judy's mum's Romani caravan close to?

5. Where was Judy's dad when she arrived home?

6. What is Alan doing when Judy first meets him?

7. Where was Judy's mum when the vicarage was bombed?

8. Why do Alan and Judy go into the crypt?

Word list

air raid: attacks from aircraft that drop bombs on planned targets

chaplain: a wartime chaplain, such as an air-force chaplain, looked after the spiritual needs of pilots and their families, for example by leading church services

crypt: a room underground, made of stone, where bodies in coffins are kept; crypts are found in places like churches or graveyards

doodlebug: (also called a buzz-bomb or a V1) a bomb like a small aircraft, with wings and an engine, but with no pilot. When it reached a targeted area, the engine stopped, and it dropped and exploded

evacuee: a person, usually a child or vulnerable person, who was offered a safer place to live, away from their home, during the war

National Restaurant: a restaurant that provided meals to people who couldn't afford food during the war or whose home had been bombed

rationing: a system introduced with ration books and vouchers to make sure that the limited amount of food available was shared around equally. This was for food in short supply, such as sugar, meat, tea and eggs

Romani caravan: a wooden van that has four wheels and a cover, lived in by Romani people. They were traditionally pulled by a horse and brightly coloured

shillings: coins worth twelve pence each that were used as currency in Britain before decimal coins (what we use today) were introduced in February 1971. There were twenty shillings in one pound

sirens: a loud emergency noise, set off when enemy aircraft were spotted, warning people that bombs might be dropped

squatting: living in a place illegally, such as a house that you don't own or pay rent for

the Underground: the network of underground trains in London. People slept overnight in the Underground stations because they felt safer from the bombs deep underground

vicarage: a house next to a church where the vicar (a Church of England priest) and his or her family live

Quick quiz answers

1. Somerset

2. Auntie Poll and Auntie Betty

3. Eggs and butter

4. Uncle Jack's house

5. Brighton

6. Lying on a tombstone, looking through binoculars

7. In the cellar

8. To shelter from a doodlebug

Super-Readable
ROLLERCOASTERS

Super-Readable Rollercoasters are an exciting new collection brought to you through a collaboration between Oxford University Press and specialist publisher Barrington Stoke. Written by bestselling and award-winning authors, these titles are intended to engage and enthuse, with themes and issues matched to the readers' age.

The books have been expertly edited to remove any barriers to comprehension and then carefully laid out in Barrington Stoke's dyslexia-friendly font to make them as accessible as possible. Their shorter length allows readers to build confidence and reading stamina while engaging in a gripping, well-told story that will ensure an enjoyable reading experience.

Other titles available in the
Super-Readable Rollercoasters series:

Dark Peak by Marcus Sedgwick
Edgar & Adolf by Phil Earle and Michael Wagg
Lightning Strike by Tanya Landman
Rat by Patrice Lawrence
I am the Minotaur by Anthony McGowan

Free online teaching resources accompany all the titles in the Super-Readable Rollercoasters series and are available from:

http://www.oxfordsecondary.com/superreadable